The
Artist's
Friends

The
Artist's Friends

written and illustrated by
Allison Barrows

Carolrhoda Books, Inc./Minneapolis

Many thanks to our good friends—the artists appearing in this book—whose work teaches some but inspires many: Jim Laurier, pages 10–11; Sharon Reuter, pages 14–15; Peter Rowe, pages 16–17; Joy Haddock, pages 18–19; Joseph DeVito Studio, pages 20–21. Special thanks to Fleet Street Publications, publishers of Discover Horses.

Carolrhoda Books, Inc., c/o The Lerner Publishing Group
241 First Avenue North, Minneapolis, Minnesota 55401 USA
Website address: www.lernerbooks.com

Library of Congress Cataloging-in-Publication Data

Barrows, Allison, 1958–
The artist's friends / written and illustrated by Allison Barrows.
p.   cm.
Summary: An aspiring artist goes with her father to meet his friends, all of whom produce different forms of art in different styles.
ISBN 1-57505-054-4
[1. Artists—Fiction.] I. Title.
PZ7.B27566Ap   1998
[Fic]—dc21   96–43533

Manufactured in the United States of America
1 2 3 4 5 6 – JR – 03 02 01 00 99 98

To future artists everywhere

For the longest time, I didn't know what I wanted to be. I thought of becoming a singer, like my mother. Or a dancer, like my ballet teacher. Or a firefighter. (My friend Max wants to be a firefighter.)

The problem was, I couldn't make up my mind.

Then one day, my father asked me to pose for one of his paintings. He's an artist. He paints pictures for the covers of books. Here's what the painting looked like before it was made into a book cover. (That's me in the middle, dressed up as a princess.)

Posing for my father and watching him paint made me
want to be an artist, too. But now I have another
problem: What kind of artist should I be?

My father says there are *many* kinds of artists. "I have
an idea," he said. "I'll take you to meet some of my artist
friends. Maybe you'll find out what kind of artist you
want to become."

First, we visited Jim, an aviation artist. He paints
pictures of old airplanes from World War II.

We watched him work on a new painting for a retired
Air Force commander. Jim paints in oil on stretched
canvas. Oil paints have a very strong smell, but I like it!
Maybe painting with oils is the thing for me.

Next, we met Leigh at an outdoor fair. She draws pictures called caricatures. People tell Leigh what they do for work or for fun. Then she draws them in a silly way. Leigh draws on paper with a thick black pen and colored markers. I love the caricatures she did of me and my father, but is this the kind of artist I want to be?

My father's friend Sharon is an art director. She works for many different people. Right now, she's designing a magazine. Sharon reads the stories, chooses typefaces, and asks photographers to take pictures. Then she puts the words and pictures on the page.

When the magazine is finished, Sharon promised to give me a copy. I can't wait to see it. I wonder if being an art director is right for me.

Peter is a digital illustrator. Instead of a paintbrush or pencil, he uses a computer to draw and paint. Peter can create a picture on the screen and then change it any way he likes.

He made this picture just for me. I think it's great, but is this the kind of art I want to make?

Joy is a portrait artist.
She works in pastel, very fine colored chalk.
She looks at photographs, and then she draws portraits as
realistically as she can.

Joy says the secret to a good portrait is to make the
people (or their pets) look better than they really do!
I'll bet I could do that, but I wonder if portraits are what
I want to draw.

   Joey is a sculptor. He creates all sorts of statues. First, he draws a sketch of what he wants to sculpt. Then he makes a little model out of clay and wire. A mold is made from the model, and a hot liquid—usually porcelain—is poured into it. When it's dry, the mold comes off, and there is Joey's statue! Sculpting looks fun. Maybe that's the kind of art I want to make.

   I ask my father who we're going to visit next. He tells me, "Just wait and see!"

When we get to my grandparents' house, I'm surprised at first. As soon as we go inside, I ask them, "Are you artists, too?"

"We were both art teachers," says Grandma. "I taught children your age in elementary school, and Grandpa taught older kids in junior high. I'll bet we could teach *you* a thing or two!"

No wonder I want to be an artist. Art is in my blood!

But what kind of artist should I be?
Should I paint planes, like Jim? Maybe my mother
would let me paint them on the walls of my little
brother's room.

Should I draw caricatures, like Leigh does? I could
draw my friends at school.

Should I learn to use the computer, like Peter? Could I work on lots of different things, like Sharon?

Could I draw
portraits of people,   or sculpt,

or teach art, like Joy or Joey or
Grandma and Grandpa?

There are so many ways
to be an artist,
I just can't decide!

I asked my father if he knew right away what kind of artist he wanted to be. "No," he said. "At first, I loved to draw comic book superheroes. When I went to art school, I learned to draw and paint other things.

"But the very first step is drawing. Draw every day, and you're on your way to becoming the artist you want to be."

"I like cats," I said. "And horses. Are those good things to draw?"

"Anything you like is a good thing to draw," said my father. "Let's find some art supplies so you can start drawing today."

We looked around the house for pencils, paints and brushes, modeling clay, colored chalk, markers, paper, scissors, and glue. We even found some corks, sponges, feathers, and wires.

I draw and paint every day now, and I'm getting better and better. I sculpt with modeling clay, and I'm learning how to use the computer. My grandparents even taught my friends and me how to make papier-mâché masks.

I still don't know what kind of artist I want to be when I grow up. Maybe I'll be *all* of them!